D0507306

Driftwood Dragons
and other seaside poems

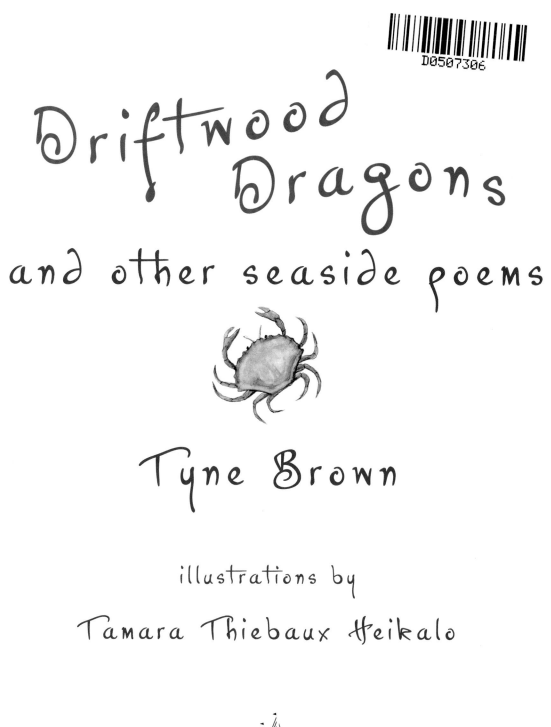

Tyne Brown

illustrations by

Tamara Thiebaux Heikalo

NIMBUS PUBLISHING

CALGARY PUBLIC LIBRARY

AUG 2012

Dedication

For Ben, Per, and Kendrick
—Tyne Brown

For my father, Martial Thiebaux, in thanks
for his enduring support and enthusiasm
for my work. *Thanks, Dad!*
—Tamara Thiebaux Heikalo

Text copyright © 2012, Tyne Brown
Illustrations copyright © 2012, Tamara Thiebaux Heikalo

All rights reserved. No part of this book may be reproduced, stored in a retrieval system or transmitted in any form or by any means without the prior written permission from the publisher, or, in the case of photocopying or other reprographic copying, permission from Access Copyright, 1 Yonge Street, Suite 1900, Toronto, Ontario M5E 1E5.

Nimbus Publishing Limited
3731 Mackintosh St, Halifax, NS B3K 5A5
(902) 455-4286 nimbus.ca

Printed and bound in Canada

Author photo: Robert Brown
Illustrator photo: Daniel Heikalo
Design: Volante Multimedia

"Enormous Whales and Tiny Snails" reprinted with permission by Children's Better Health Institute; copyright © 2003 *Turtle Magazine for Preschool Kids*.

Library and Archives Canada Cataloguing in Publication

Brown, Tyne
Driftwood dragons : and other seaside poems / Tyne Brown ; illustrated by Tamara Thiébaux-Heikalo.
ISBN 978-1-55109-893-7

I. Thiébaux-Heikalo, Tamara II. Title.
PS8603.R696D75 2012   jC811'.6   C2011-907617-9

The Canada Council | Le Conseil des Arts
for the Arts | du Canada

NOVA SCOTIA
Communities, Culture and Heritage

Nimbus Publishing acknowledges the financial support for its publishing activities from the Government of Canada through the Canada Book Fund (CBF) and the Canada Council for the Arts, and from the Province of Nova Scotia through the Department of Communities, Culture and Heritage.

For whatever we lose (like a you or a me)
It's always ourselves we find in the sea

—Edward Estlin Cummings

The Perfect Pebble

Pebbles galore
Lie along the shore
Scattered on the sand,

And I love to search
For the perfect one and
Hold it in my hand.

I drop it in my pocket,
And take it home with me.
Now every time I touch it

I hear and smell the sea.

The Beach Flea*

The beach flea isn't snazzy bright,
He hasn't set the world alight,
He doesn't sing or dance or write,
But when he jumps
He's out of . . . . sight.
He never makes a mighty roar,
No one's even heard him snore,
He just lives quietly by the shore,
But when he leaps
You'll see him soar!
Now you may think he's just a gnat,
An unimportant one at that,
But in his sandy habitat
He's an Olympic acrobat!

* The beach flea, also known as a sand hopper, and sand flea, is actually not a flea at all, but a crustacean related to other crustaceans such as crabs and shrimp.

Two Moons

In starry dark,
In midnight sky,
The silvery moon
Glides slowly by.

In starlit bays,
Between moon tides,
On silvery sands
The Moon Snail glides.

New Day

Swooping swallows,
Sweeping sand,
Ocean fingers
Reach for land.

Sparkling sun,
Seashine bright,
Sunrise spreading
Morning light.

Ruddy Turnstones
Dot the shore,
Seaweed hugs
The ocean floor.

Each fresh morning
Dawns anew,
Each new day
A gift for you.

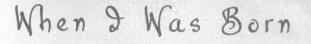

When I Was Born

When I was born
I never knew
The sky was high,
The ocean blue,
That tides rolled in
And flowed back out,
That Moon pulled the sea
As it travelled about.

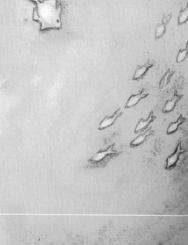

When I was born
I did not know
That great whales lived
Down deep below,
Or that the creatures
Of the sea
Shared this world
With you and me.

Shape Shifters

Clouds
drift, shift,
spread, lift,
zoom, loom,
scud, plume,
curl, swirl,
roll, twirl,
sweep, heap,
wisp and creep.
But when those
shape shifters,
rain sifters,
snow spreaders,
hail shedders
disappear—

The sailing is clear!

There's Only One You

There are catfish and flatfish and jellyfish, too,
There are all kinds of fish, but there's only one you.

And all of the wondrous fish in the sea,
Can't be as special as you are to me.

Music by the Sea

Listen to the plovers as
They pipe along the shore,
Listen to the roll of stones
Drum the ocean floor.
Listen to the brassy cry
Of gulls above the docks,
Listen to percussion waves
Crash against the rocks.
Listen to the orchestra
That plays beside the ocean.
Just be still and you will hear
A symphony in motion.

Seal Play

Seal wanders down under,
Down under, down under,
She wanders down under
The beautiful sea.
And what does she see there?
She sees a sea fair,
A magical sea fair!
Admission is free.

A starfish who lights up
The water each day,
A blowfish who keeps
All the dust blown away,
A shellfish who walks around
Every which way—
Such wonders Seal sees
In the deep sea each day!

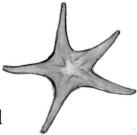

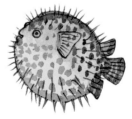

Sky Fishing

Benjamin Lee went down to the sea
And cast his net up high.
He thought it was fun to fish for the sun
That swam in a cloudy sky.

He hauled in his net, now dew-drop wet,
With a hey and a hi-heave-ho,
Then he blinked his eyes in great surprise,
For he'd caught a fresh rainbow!

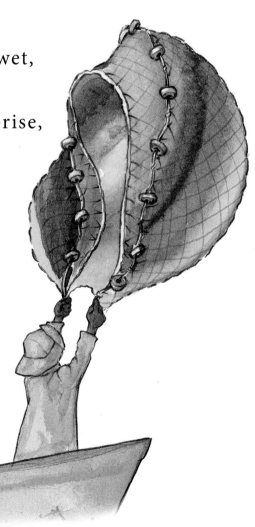

Enormous Whales
and
Tiny Snails

Enormous whales can flip their tails,
And make some thunderous whacks!
While tiny snails make silent trails,
Toting seashells on their backs.

14

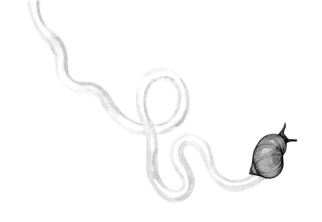

Small Talk

"What are you doing, Little Snail?"
"Making a trail."

Just Wondering

Sea, do you ever
get tired from running
in and out all the time?

Sandpipers

Sandpipers skimming the ocean in flight
Where did you learn to wheel left and right?
Where did you learn to fly in formation,
Wingtip to wingtip without hesitation?

Where did you learn such coordination?

Where did you learn to speed up as one,
Like a gossamer cloth spun from the sun;
To dive and to dip in an aerial feat,
To perform like a troupe of the flying elite?

Where did you learn such cooperation?

Flight school, perhaps, or the National Ballet?
Maybe you trained with the Cirque du Soleil.
Or did your skill come from a place deep within
Where all our accomplishments usually begin?

Morning on Martinique Beach

Ocean
Rises from her
Sandy bed
And shakes her
Sheets in waves
Of brisk wind.
See how they billow
In the breeze.

Shell Song

Sing me a lullaby, seashell,
Softly whisper a song
Of ships and sails and humpback whales
And I will dream along.

Let me drift with you to sea,
And sail my whole life long,
As over the waves I roam the world
On a seashell's dream-along song.

Driftwood Dragons

Driftwood dragons doze
on sun-warmed rocks, too lazy
to get up and run.

Star Wish Starfish

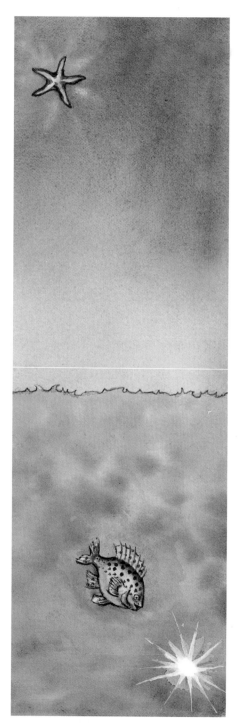

Does a starfish ever wish
On a star?
Does he wish
He could travel afar?
Would he like to fly high
Through a star-studded sky
And shine upon Zanzibar?

Does a star ever wish
On a starfish?
Does she wish
She could splash, splosh, and splish?
Would she like to be free
To dive in the sea
And swim with a polka-dot fish?

Well, stars in the sky
Are perfect for wishes,
While stars in the sea
Make perfect starfishes,
So each in its place,
Just where it should be,
Stars in the sky and stars in the sea.

Fundy Jellies

Jellyfish float like
open umbrellas in one
big ocean puddle.

Dawn

Morning star and moon,
together in one big sky—
such a brief moment.

Seashore Whimsy

Today I think I'd like to be
A jumping, leaping, small beach flea.
I'll hop and skip across the sand
And be so small, yet feel so grand!

Or maybe I will try to fly,
Like a seagull in the sky.
I'll swoop and loop and have such fun,
A tiny speck up by the sun.

But when I touch down on the ground
With arms held wide I'll spin around,
Like seaweed swaying to and fro,
I'll swirl and twirl on tippy-toe.

Some Like It Hot
Some Like It Cold

People will say, "It's delightful today!"
Whenever it's hot, dry, and sunny,
But fish in the sea beg to disagree,
And much prefer cold, wet, and runny!

Ocean Playground

Small waves splash naked
in the sea until wind puts
white caps on their heads.

Mystery at Lawrencetown Beach

Is that a seal or a surfer swimming in the sea
sporting such a sleek black suit?

Seaweed Garden

There is a garden in my yard
I have to dig and hoe,
But by the sea a special kind
Of garden seems to grow.

I never have to tend to it,
There's nothing to maintain,
Just swirls of graceful seaweed,
Like frost upon a pane.

And when the ocean harvests it
And takes it out to sea,
It always finds its way again
Back in to shore and me.

Hot Day at the Beach

Beach umbrellas bloom in the sand like dandelions sprouting in a sea of grass.

Deep Freeze

Hot day.
Hot sun,
Hot sand,
Quick, run—
Ocean blue,
So nice,
Jump in,
Like ice!

Sambro Head

Fireflies,
Lighthouse,
Ships in the night,
Blinking and glowing
Luminous bright,
Sending light messages far and near
In starlit dark, "See me, I'm here."

Shore Pearls

Bayberries, little
silver pearls
adorn drab and barren
winter fields.

One Bright Spot

Grey are the ships, the sea, the sky,
And the shore so foggy and long.
The only thing bright in this day's
Misty light is the meadowlark's
Musical song.

My Friend Is Gone

The foghorn sounds so low and long,
Waves lap on the shore.
Great whales sing their mournful song.
My friend isn't here anymore.

Sea Fields

Strawberries wild,
Warm in the sun,
First taste of summer,
Now winter is done.

Picture Perfect

Lupins sing
Their pink
And purple
Songs,
Splashing
The fields
With pitch-perfect
Colour.

Osprey

Floating over the ocean like a kite
on an invisible string,
osprey takes
a sudden
tailspin
dive
and

p
l
u
m
m
e
t
s

into the sea.

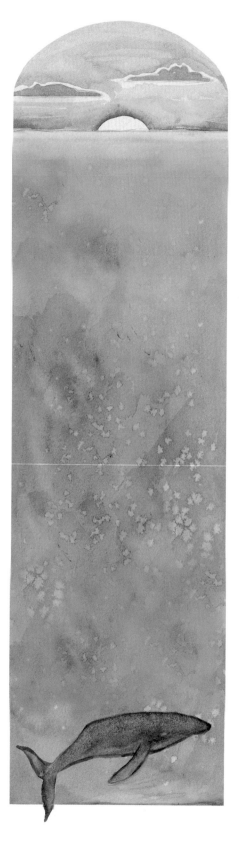

Touch a Wish

If you could hear the leaves
Change from green to orange and red,
Or hear the silver moon
As it floats up overhead,
Would you stop and listen
To what was being said?

If you could see the buzz
Of a busy bumblebee,
Or see the song a whale sings
While swimming in the sea,
What a different kind of world
This world would surely be.

If you could touch a poem,
A wish, a hope, a song,
Would you touch them gently,
Let them go where they belong?
If you could hear the sunrise
As it spreads above the sea,

What a different kind of world
This world would surely be.